This book belongs to

_____

_____

Alex Hears God's Voice

SUJATHA SEKHAR

Email : support@sujisfinds.com

ISBN 979-8-9873098-0-3 (paperback)

Printed in the U.S.A
First Printing, January 2023

www.sujisfinds.com

Dedicated to God and All Children

Alex and Rex were best friends.
Every day, they rode the school bus together.

One day, Alex got on the school bus
and sat next to Rex.
"Hi, Rex," said Alex. Rex was silent.

Alex held Rex's hand and said,
"How are you feeling today?"
"I'm all right," replied Rex.

PARK ⬆

"I can't wait to visit the science museum with you,"
Alex said. Rex remained quiet.
Rex is sad. I'll pray to God for him, thought Alex.
"Rex, can I pray for you?" Alex asked.
"Sure!" said Rex.

Alex prayed,
"Dear Father,
who is in heaven,
You are our provider.
Provide for Rex's family.
Take care of all their needs.
Fill Rex with peace and joy.
In Jesus' name, I pray. Amen."

"Thank you!" said Rex. "Alex, I am happy now."
"Children, get off the bus," said the bus driver.
Alex and Rex had fun at school that day.

Three days later, Alex hopped on the school bus and sat next to Rex. "Hello, Alex!" said Rex.

"When I was sad last Friday, you mentioned my family problem during prayer. How did you know that?"

Alex replied, "You had a gloomy face. I was sorry for you. So, I prayed to God for you. Then, the Holy Spirit revealed in my heart that your family situation was bothering you. He also urged me to pray with you."

"My dad lost his job a month ago," Rex said. "He told my mom that he didn't have enough money to pay all the bills."

"God will meet all your needs," Alex assured Rex.
"You're right, Alex!" Rex exclaimed. "You prayed
and God did a miracle. On Monday, my dad got
a new job. Today is his first day at work."

"What a wonderful miracle!" Alex rejoiced. "When you prayed to God, you heard His voice in your heart," said Rex. "That's awesome!"

The bus arrived at the school.
Students walked to their classrooms.

Alex and Rex had fun during recess.
Then, they had lunch together.
"Alex! Let's buy ice cream," said Rex.

Alex and Rex ate their favorite ice cream.
"Rex! Thanks for the tasty treat," said Alex.
"It was delicious!"

About the Author

Sujatha Sekhar grew up in a non-Christian family in India. After committing her life to Jesus as a teenager, she spent more time studying the Bible. The Holy Spirit inspired her to write Bible-based children's stories. She previously worked in IT industry before transitioning to children's book publishing. She lives in Charlotte, North Carolina with her husband, Robert, and their two children.

You can contact Sujatha at @sujathasekhar on Instagram, or check out her website at www.sujisfinds.com.

Made in the USA
Middletown, DE
28 January 2023

23449353R00018